D0550862

CHANGE-A-LOT   COOLEST RULEST   IN NAPPI

First published by Hamish Hamilton Children's Books 1988
First published in Picture Lions 1990
Picture Lions is an imprint of the Children's Division,
part of the Collins Publishing Group,
8 Grafton Street, London W1X 3LA

Copyright © 1988 by Babette Cole

Printed and bound by Warners of Bourne and London

King Change-a-lot
by
Babette Cole

COLLINS
PICTURE LIONS

Prince Change-a-lot was fed up with being treated like a baby.

His parents, King and Queen Spend-fortune, were making a bad job of running the kingdom and everyone was complaining.

They spent the people's taxes on silly parties and expensive clothes.

They hardly ever saw Prince Change-a-lot, who was looked after by Miss Grumpbladder, the court nanny.

There was a plot to blow up the government offices
because nobody was governing properly . . .

and big hairy giants were kicking down castles left, right and centre . . .

. . . and the bad fairies were cooking up
some rotten spells,

so the good fairies had gone on strike!

To make matters worse, the dragons were rampaging all over the place, and flying off with maidens belonging to the neighbouring kingdoms!

There was a plague of disgusting blubber worms who were eating all the crops.

But the King and Queen did not want to hear about anything so distasteful.

Nor did they want to hear about the bad behaviour
in the kingdom's boring old schools.

"I'd change a few things around here,"
said Prince Change-a-lot,
"if only I could talk
like a grown-up."

One day he saw the court magician making
a genie appear by rubbing a pot.
The genie could grant wishes.

He tried the same trick on his own potty and out came a baby genie who could understand baby language!

"Leave it all up to me,"
said the baby genie.

The baby genie whizzed over Prince Change-a-lot . . .

BLAH BLAH
BLAH
BLAH

. . . and Prince Change-a-lot
started to talk like
the Prime Minister!

The baby genie whizzed over Change-a-lot's parents.

Two minutes later they were behaving like
the worst kind of babies themselves!

The baby genie whizzed back into the potty.
"OK," said Prince Change-a-lot,
"I'm King now!"

The first thing he did was to give his
parents to Nanny Grumpbladder.

Then he turned the government offices into a
gigantic fun-fair so that nobody wanted
to blow it up.

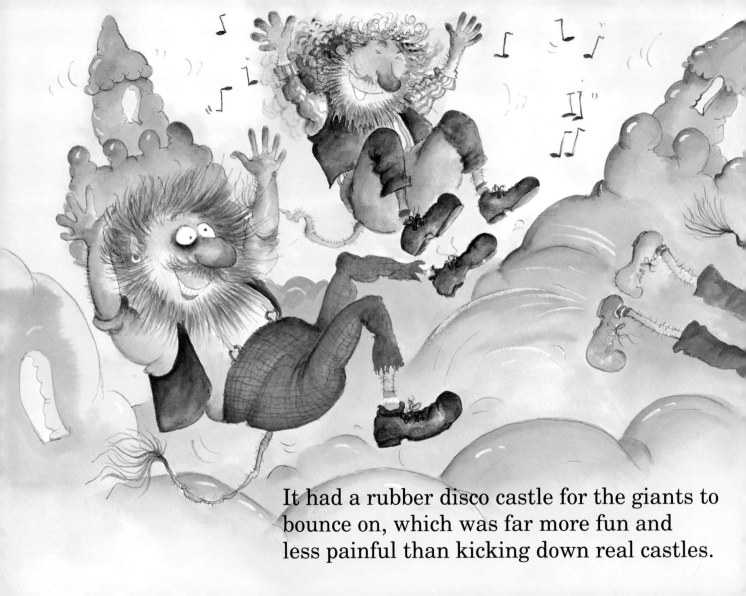

It had a rubber disco castle for the giants to bounce on, which was far more fun and less painful than kicking down real castles.

King Change-a-lot had all the bad
fairies locked up so that the
good fairies could get back to work.

He gave the dragons video games to play so that they would stay at home.

The neighbours were pleased to pay the new king for keeping the dragons away.

With the money, he bought lorryloads of cakes and jellies . . .

. . . which he fed to the disgusting blubber worms,
who ate so much jelly they just exploded!

Finally, he closed down all the boring old schools because he didn't want to go to one . . .

and he didn't want to send his parents to one either!

King Change-a-lot lived to be a very
popular and clever monarch . . .
. . . with the help of his potty!